W9-BUO-007

Cinderdog
AND THE
Wicked Stepcat

HEN

E

WRITTEN AND ILLUSTRATED BY
Joan Holub

Albert Whitman & Company

Morton Grove, Illinois

For the mighty fine buckaroos at Albert Whitman,
with special thanks to Abby, Kathy, and Scott. – J. H.

Library of Congress Cataloging-in-Publication Data

Holub, Joan.

Cinderdog and the wicked stepcat / written and illustrated by Joan Holub.

p. cm.

Summary: When Cowboy Carl marries Cactus Kate, Carl's dog
Cinderdog must deal with his new sibling, Kate's ornery cat Wicked.

ISBN 0-8075-1178-1

[1. Dogs – Fiction. 2. Cats – Fiction. 3. Cowboys – Fiction. 4. West (U.S.) – Fiction.] I. Title.

PZ7.H7427 Ci 2001 [E] – dc21   00-010206

The paintings were done using watercolor,

acrylic, and gouache on Arches 140-pound watercolor paper.

The typefaces used are LoType and RioChico.

The design is by Scott Piehl.

Yee-hah!

Way out west, near a ripsnortin' town you never heard of, there once lived a critter name of Cinderdog and his best bud, Cowboy Carl.

Every day, the two pardners worked the
Gitalong Ranch from sunup to sundown.

The Gitalong Ranch

On clear nights, they sang campfire ditties and bunked down under the stars. 'Long about midnight, Cowboy Carl would give Cinderdog a pat and say, "Good dog, Cinder." And they would drift off to sleep.

Just the two of them.

But one day, trouble came rollin' in.
It was Cactus Kate and her ornery furball, Wicked.

In two shakes of a rattler's tail, Cowboy Carl was thinkin' on makin' Cactus Kate his wife.

Cinderdog tried to explain to Cowboy Carl that this was pretty nigh on to the worst idea he had ever had. Even worse than the time he tried to lasso a skunk.

But sometimes Cowboy Carl didn't have a whole lot of horse sense. He got himself all gussied up, and there was a weddin', lickety-split.

Cinderdog got a brand-spankin'-new
stepmother, and a Stepcat to boot.
Whether he liked it or not.

Turns out that Cactus Kate had more fussy rules than you could shake a stick at.

And Cowboy Carl? Why, he was so busy moonin' and spoonin' that he hardly paid his chores any mind at all.

Rules for Cinderdog:
No mud tracks
No loud barking
No drooling
No cat-chasing
No sock-chewing
(continued on back)

Rules for Wicked:
Anything Goes!

Somebody had to take up the slack. It seemed all Cinderdog did was work, work, work.

Did Cactus Kate's pesky varmint pitch in and help?
Not hardly. That great big tumbleweed of a cat was
called Wicked, and her name fit her fine.

Cinderdog

"Try to make Kate's kitty feel welcome," Cowboy Carl told Cinderdog. "We want you both to be friends."

Friends? Now Cinderdog knew Cowboy Carl had gone plumb loco.

That cat was enough to make anyone dog-tired.

When Cinderdog said *howdy,* Wicked Stepcat hissed.

She liked to share.
His food.

And she scratched purt near everything. Includin' Cinderdog.

Yup. Two was company.
But *four* was a crowd.

Don't The Gitalong Ranch

One mornin', Cowboy Carl, Cactus Kate, and Wicked Stepcat saddled up and hit the trail.

"We're off to the cat show! Watch the ranch, pardner!" Cowboy Carl hollered back at him.

Cinderdog was left
behind, eatin' their dust.

Fancy Schmancy
Cat Show

Prizes Galore:

Sparkly Cat Collars
Newfangled Cat Toys
Hissy Prissy Cat Chow

Sponsored by
Yippee-yi-yo Pet Stores
(No Dogs Allowed.)

Jumpin' junebugs! Cowboy Carl
loved his new family more than he
loved Cinderdog. That was certain.

Cinderdog lit out for the cat show to tell Cowboy Carl so long forever. He wasn't playin' second fiddle to a cat!

A rascally windstorm pestered him a mite along the way.

By the time he arrived, he was so messed up he looked like a cat!

He went inside and took a load off. Quicker than lightnin', some city slickers were sizin' him up. Then they slapped a ribbon on him. Danged if he hadn't gone and won a prize at the cat show! It was humiliatin'.

Sudden-like, Cinderdog noticed a sneaky desperado headin' his way. It looked like he was up to no good.

Sure enough, that lowdown desperado stuffed Wicked
and Cinderdog into his saddlebag and took off for the
desert!

"You two varmints will make mighty tasty snacks
for my pet snake, Fang," he told them.

After a bumpy ride, the desperado let his two "cats" out of the bag. Only then he saw that Cinderdog actually 'twernt a cat at all!

Cinderdog let out his fiercest growl,
and the desperado headed for the hills.

Did Wicked Stepcat have a kind word for Cinderdog after he'd saved her hide? Not likely.

Instead she said, "I want to go home. Back where Kate and I used to live."

Cinderdog was confounded. "You don't like the ranch?"

Wicked sniffled and looked sorta weepy. "How would you like it if *you* had to leave the Gitalong Ranch and move to somebody else's house?"

Right then and there Cinderdog began to see Wicked Stepcat's side of things.

After they had chewed the fat for a spell longer, she began to see his side, too. By sunrise, they were purt near buddies.

They headed for the ranch, where Cowboy Carl and Cactus Kate seemed right glad to see them both.

From that day on, Cinderdog tried to make Wicked Stepcat feel at home on the ranch.

He showed her how to keep the cows in line. She didn't really get the hang of it, but Cinderdog didn't let on.

In return, Wicked Stepcat let Cinderdog play with her best toys. First he drooled on them, then he buried them. But Wicked didn't twitch a whisker.

'Round about midnight every night, Cowboy Carl and Cactus Kate would give Cinderdog and Wicked Stepcat each a pat. And they would say, "Good dog, Cinder. Good cat, Wicked."

Yessiree, Bob. Life on the Gitalong was good once again.
They were a happy bunch.
Just the four of them.

But then . . .
    one day . . .
        in a cloud of trail dust . . .

Trouble with a capital "T" came ridin' in.

It was the rootin', tootin', orneriest critter Cinderdog
and Wicked Stepcat had ever laid eyes on.
It was louder than a summer cyclone.
It was wilder than a desert coyote.
It was (gasp!) . . .

...COWBABY!